CRY FROM
a Far Planet

CRY FROM
a Far Planet
Tom Godwin

ÆGYPAN PRESS

this story first appeared in the September, 1958, issue of
Amazing Science Fiction Stories.

Special thanks to Greg Weeks, Stephen Blundell, and the
Online Distributed Proofreading Team (which can be found
at http://www.pgdp.net).

Cry from a Far Planet
A publication of
ÆGYPAN PRESS

www.aegypan.com

The problem of separating the friends from the enemies was a major one in the conquest of space as many a dead spacer could have testified. A tough job when you could see an alien and judge appearances; far tougher when they were only whispers on the wind.

A smile of friendship is a baring of the teeth. So is a snarl of menace. It can be fatal to mistake the latter for the former.

Harm an alien being only under circumstances of self-defense.

TRUST NO ALIEN BEING UNDER ANY CIRCUMSTANCES.

— From *Exploration Ship's Handbook*

*H*e listened in the silence of the Exploration ship's control room. He heard nothing but that was what bothered him; an ominous quiet when there should have been a multitude of sounds from the nearby village for the viewscreen's audio-pickups to transmit. And it was more than six hours past the time when the native,

Throon, should have come to sit with him outside the ship as they resumed the laborious attempt to learn each other's language.

The viewscreen was black in the light of the control room, even though it was high noon outside. The dull red sun was always invisible through the world's thick atmosphere and to human eyes full day was no more than a red-tinged darkness.

He switched on the ship's outside floodlights and the viewscreen came to bright white life, showing the empty glades reaching away between groves of purple alien trees. He noticed, absently, that the trees seemed to have changed a little in color since his arrival.

The village was hidden from view by the outer trees but there should have been some activity in the broad area visible to him. There was none, not even along the distant segment of what should have been a busy road. The natives were up to something and he knew, from hard experience on other alien worlds, that it would be nothing good. It would be another misunderstanding of some kind and he didn't know enough of their incomprehensible language to ask them what it was —

*S*uddenly, as it always came, he felt someone or something standing close behind him and peering over his shoulder. He dropped his hand to the blaster he had taken to wearing at all times and whirled.

Nothing was behind him. There never was. The control room was empty, with no hiding place for anything, and the door was closed, locked by the remote-control button beside him. There was nothing.

The sensation of being watched faded, as though the watcher had withdrawn to a greater distance. It was perhaps the hundredth time within six days that he had felt the sensation. And when he slept at night something came to nuzzle at his mind; faceless, formless, utterly alien. For the past three nights he had not let the blaster get beyond quick reach of his hand, even when in bed.

But whatever it was, it could not be on the ship. He had searched the ship twice, a methodical compartment-by-compartment search that had found nothing. It had to be the work of the natives from outside the ship. Except. . . .

Why, if the natives were telepathic, did the one called Throon go through the weary pretense of trying to learn a mutually understandable form of communication?

There was one other explanation, which he could not accept: that he was following in the footsteps of Will Garret of Ship Nine who had deliberately gone into a white sun two months after the death of his twin brother.

He looked at the chair beside his own, Johnny's chair, which would forever be empty, and his thoughts went back down the old, bitter paths. The Exploration Board had been wrong when they thought the close bond between identical twins would make them the ideal two-man crews for the lonely, lifetime journeys of the Exploration Ships. Identical twins were too close; when one of them died, the other died in part with him.

They had crossed a thousand light-years of space together, he and Johnny, when they came to the bleak planet that he would name Johnny's World. He should never have let Johnny go alone up the slope of the honey-combed mountain — but Johnny had wanted to take the routine record photographs of the black, tigerlike beasts which they had called cave cats and the things had seemed harmless and shy, despite their ferocious appearance.

"I'm taking them a sack of food that I think they might like," Johnny had said. "I want to try to get some good close-up shots of them."

Ten minutes later he heard the distant snarl of Johnny's blaster. He ran up the mountainside, knowing already that he was too late. He found two of the cave cats lying where Johnny had killed them. Then he found Johnny, at the foot of a high cliff. He was dead, his neck broken by the fall. Scattered all around him from the torn sack was the food he had wanted to give to the cats.

He buried Johnny the next day, while a cold wind moaned under a lead-grey sky. He built a monument for him; a little mound of frosty stones that only the wild animals would ever see —

A chime rang, high and clear, and the memories were shattered. The orange light above the hyperspace communicator was flashing; the signal that meant the Exploration Board was calling him from Earth.

He flipped the switch and said, "Paul Jameson, Exploration Ship One."

The familiar voice of Brender spoke:

"It's been some time since your preliminary report. Is everything all right?"

"In a way," he answered. "I was going to give you the detailed report tomorrow."

"Give me a brief sketch of it now."

"Except for their short brown fur, the natives are humanoid in appearance. But there are basic differences. Their body temperature is cool, like their climate. Their vision range is from just within the visible red on into the infrared. They'll shade their eyes from the light of anything as hot as boiling water but they'll look square into the ship's floodlights and never see them."

"And their knowledge of science?" Brender asked.

"They have a good understanding of it, but along lines entirely different from what our own were at their stage of development. For example: they power their machines with chemicals but there is no steam, heat, or exhaust."

"That's what we want to find — worlds where branches of research unknown to our science are being explored. How about their language?"

"No progress with it yet." He told Brender of the silence in the village and added, "Even if Throon should show up I could not ask him what was wrong. I've learned a few words but they have so many different definitions that I can't use them."

"I know," Brender said. "Variable and unrelated definitions, undetectable shades of inflection — and sometimes a language that has no discernibly separate words. The Singer brothers of Ship Eight ran into the latter. We've given them up as lost."

"The Singers — dead?" he exclaimed. "Good God — it's been only a month since the Ramon brothers were killed."

"The circumstances were similar," Brender said. "They always are. There is no way the Exploration men can tell the natives that they mean them no harm and the suspicion of the natives grows into dangerous hostility. The Singers reported the natives on that world to be both suspicious and possessing powerful weapons. The Singers were proceeding warily, their own weapons always at hand. But, somehow, the natives caught them off-guard — their last report was four months ago."

There was a silence, then Brender added, "Their ship was the ninth — and we had only fifteen."

He did not reply to the implications of Brender's statement. It was obvious to them all what the end of the Plan would be. What it had to be.

*I*t had been only three years since the fifteen heavily armed Exploration ships set out to lead the way for

Terran expansion across the galaxy; to answer a cry from far planets, and to find all the worlds that held intelligent life. That was the ultimate goal of the Plan: to accumulate and correlate all the diverse knowledge of all the intelligent life-forms in the galaxy. Among the achievements resulting from that tremendous mass of data would be a ship's drive faster even than hyperspace; the Third Level Drive which would bring all the galaxies of the universe within reach.

And now nine ships were gone out of fifteen and nineteen men out of thirty. . . .

"The communication barrier," Brender said. "The damned communication barrier has been the cause behind the loss of every ship. And there is nothing we can do about it. We're stymied by it. . . ."

The conversation was terminated shortly afterward and he moved about the room restlessly, wishing it was time to lift ship again. With Johnny not there the dark world was like a smothering tomb. He would like to leave it behind and drive again into the star clouds of the galaxy; drive on and on into them —

A ghostly echo touched his mind; restless, poignantly yearning. He swung to face the locked door, knowing there could be nothing behind it. The first real fear came to him as he did so. The thing was lonely — the thing that watched him was as lonely as he was. . . .

What else could any of it be but the product of a mind in the first stage of insanity?

*T*he natives came ten minutes later.

The viewscreen showed their chemically-powered vehicle emerge from the trees and roll swiftly across the glade. Four natives were in it while a fifth one lay on the floor, apparently badly injured.

The vehicle stopped a short distance in front of the airlock and he recognized the native on the floor. It was Throon, the one with whom he had been exchanging language lessons.

They were waiting for him when he emerged from the ship, pistollike weapons in their belts and grim accusation in their manner.

Throon was muttering unintelligibly, unconscious. His skin, where not covered by the brown fur, was abnormal in appearance. He was dying.

The leader of the four indicated Throon and said in a quick, brittle voice: *"Ko reegar feen no-dran!"*

Only one word was familiar: *Ko,* which meant "you" and "yesterday" and a great many other things. The question was utterly meaningless to him.

He dropped his hand a little nearer his blaster as the leader spoke again; a quick succession of unknown words that ended with a harshly demanding *"kreson!"*

Kreson meant "now," or "very quickly." All the other words were unfamiliar to him. They waited, the grim menace about them increasing when he did not answer. He tried in vain to find some way of explaining to them he was not responsible for Throon's sickness and could not cure it.

Then he saw the spray of leaves that had caught on the corner of the vehicle when it came through the farther trees.

They were of a deep purple color. All the trees around the ship were almost grey by contrast.

Which meant that he *was* responsible for Throon's condition.

The cold white light of the ship's floodlights, under which he and Throon had sat for day after day, contained radiations that went through the violet and far into the ultraviolet. To the animal and vegetable life of the dark world such radiations were invisibly short and deadly.

Throon was dying of hard-radiation sickness.

It was something he should have foreseen and avoided — and that would not have happened had he accepted old Throon's pantomimed invitation, in the beginning, to go with him into the village to work at the language study. There he would have used a harmless battery lamp for illumination . . . but there was no certainty that the natives were not planning to lay a trap for him in the village and he had refused to go.

It did not matter — there was a complex radiation-neutralizer and cell-reconstructor in the ship which would return Throon to full, normal health a few hours after he was placed in its chamber.

He turned to the leader of the four natives and motioned from Throon to the airlock. "Go — there," he said in the native language.

"Bron!" the leader answered. The word meant "No" and there was a determination in the way he said it that showed he would not move from it.

At the end of five minutes his attempts to persuade them to take Throon into the ship had increased their suspicion of his motives to the point of critical danger. If only he could tell them *why* he wanted Throon taken into the ship . . . But he could not and would have to take Throon by first disposing of the four without injuring them. This he could do by procuring one of the paralyzing needle-guns from the ship.

He took a step toward the ship and spoke the words that to the best of his knowledge meant: "I come back."

"Feswin ilt k'la."

Their reply was to snatch at their weapons in desperate haste, even as the leader uttered a hoarse word of command. He brought up the blaster with the quick motion that long training had perfected and their weapons were only half drawn when his warning came:

"Bron!"

*T*hey froze, but did not release their weapons. He walked backward to the airlock, his blaster covering them, the tensely waiting manner in which they watched his progress telling him that the slightest relaxation of his vigilance would mean his death. He did not let the muzzle of the blaster waver until he was inside the airlock and the outer door had slid shut.

He was sure that the natives would be gone when he returned. And he was sure of another thing: That whatever he had said to them, it was not what he had thought he was saying.

He saw that the glade was empty when he opened the airlock again. At the same time a bomblike missile struck the ship just above the airlock and exploded with a savage crash. He jabbed the *Close* button and the door clicked shut barely in advance of three more missiles which hammered at its impervious armor.

So that, he thought wearily, is that.

He laid the useless needle-gun aside. The stage was past when he could hope to use it. He could save Throon only by killing some of the others — or he could lift ship and leave Throon to die. Either action would make the natives hate and fear Terrans; a hatred and fear that would be there to greet all future Terran ships.

That was not the way a race gave birth to peaceful galactic empire, was not the purpose behind the Plan. But always, wherever the Exploration men went, they encountered the deadly barrier; the intangible, unassailable communication barrier. With the weapons an Exploration man carried in his ship he had the power to destroy a world — but not the power to ask the simple questions that would prevent fatal misunderstandings.

And before another three years had passed the last Exploration man would die, the last Exploration ship would be lost.

He felt the full force of hopelessness for the first time. When Johnny had been alive it had been different; Johnny, who had laughed whenever the outlook was the darkest and said, *"We'll find a way, Paul —"*

The thought broke as suddenly, unexpectedly, he felt that Johnny was very near. With the feeling came the soft enclosure of a dreamlike peace in which Johnny's death was vague and faraway; only something that had happened in another dream. He knew, without wondering why, that Johnny was in the control room.

A part of his mind tried to reject the thought as an illusion. He did not listen — he did not want to listen. He ran to the ship's elevator, stumbling like one not fully awake. Johnny was waiting for him in the control room — alive — alive —

*H*e spoke as he stepped into the control room:
"Johnny —"

Something moved at the control board, black and alien, standing tall as a man on short hind legs. Yellow eyes blazed in a feline face.

It was a cave cat, like the ones that had killed Johnny.

Realization was a wrenching shock and a terrible disillusionment. Johnny was not waiting for him — not alive —

He brought up the blaster, the dreamlike state gone. The paw of the cave cat flashed out and struck the ship's master light switch with a movement faster than his own. The room was instantly, totally, dark.

He fired and pale blue fire lanced across the room, to reveal that the cave cat was gone. He fired again, quickly and immediately in front of him. The pale beam revealed only the ripped metal floor.

"I am not where you think."

The words spoke clearly in his mind but there was no directional source. He held his breath, listening for the whisper of padded feet as the cave cat flashed in for the kill, and made a swift analysis of the situation.

The cave cat was telepathic and highly intelligent and had been on the ship all the time. It and the others had wanted the ship and had killed Johnny to reduce opposition to the minimum. He, himself, had been permitted to live until the cave cat learned from his mind how to operate the almost-automatic controls. Now, he had served his purpose —

"You are wrong."

Again there was no way he could determine the direction from which the thought came. He listened again, and wondered why it had not waylaid him at the door.

Its thought came:

"I had to let you see me or you would not have believed I existed. It was only here that I could extinguish all lights and have time to speak before you killed me. I let you think your brother was here. . . ." There was a little pause. *"I am sorry. I am sorry. I should have used some other method of luring you here."*

He swung the blaster toward what seemed to be a faint sound near the astrogator unit across the room.

"We did not intend to kill your brother."

He did not believe it and did not reply.

"When we made first telepathic contact with him, he jerked up his blaster and fired. In his mind was the conviction that we had pretended to be harmless animals so that we could catch him off-guard and kill him. One of us leaped at him as he fired the second time, to knock the blaster from his hand. We needed only a few minutes in which to explain — but he would not trust us that long. There was a misjudgment of distance and he was knocked off the cliff."

Again he did not reply.

"We did not intend to kill your brother," the thought came, *"but you do not believe me."*

*H*e spoke for the first time. "No, I don't believe you. You are physically like cats and cats don't misjudge distances. Now, you want something from me before you try to kill me, too. What is it?"

"I will have to tell you of my race for you to understand. We call ourselves the Varn, in so far as it can be translated into a spoken word, and we are a very old race. In the beginning we did not live in caves but there came a long period of time, for thousands of years, when the climate on our world was so violent that we were forced to live in the caves. It was completely dark there but our sense of smell became very acute, together with sufficient sensitivity to temperature changes that we could detect objects in our immediate vicinity. There were subterranean plants in the caves and food was no problem."

*"W*e had always been slightly telepathic and it was during our long stay in the caves that our intelligence and telepathic powers*

became fully developed. We had only our minds — physical science is not created in dark caves with clumsy paws.

"The time finally came when we could leave the caves but it was of little help to us. There were no resources on our world but earth and stone and the thin grass of the plains. We wondered about the universe and we knew the stars were distant suns because one of our own suns became a star each winter. We studied as best we could but we could see the stars only as the little wild animals saw them. There was so much we wanted to learn and by then we were past our zenith and already dying out. But our environment was a prison from which we could never escape.

"When your ship arrived we thought we might soon be free. We wanted to ask you to take some of us with you and arrange for others of your race to stop by on our world. But you dismissed us as animals, useful only for making warm fur coats, because we lived in caves and had no science, no artifacts — nothing. You had the power to destroy us and we did not know what your reaction would be when you learned we were intelligent and telepathic. A telepathic race must have a high code of ethics and never intrude unwanted — but would you have believed that?"

He did not answer.

"The death of your brother changed everything. You were going to leave so soon that there would be no time to learn more about you. I hid on the ship so I could study you and wait until I could prove to you that you needed me. Now, I can — Throon is dying *and I can give you the proper words of explanation that will cause the others to bring him into the ship."*

"Your real purpose — what is it?" he asked.

"To show you that men need the Varn. You want to explore the galaxy, and learn. So do the Varn. You have the ships and we have the telepathic ability that will end the communication problem. Your race and mine can succeed only if we go together."

He searched for the true, and hidden, purpose behind the Varn proposal and saw what it would have to be.

"The long-range goal — you failed to mention that . . . your ultimate aim."

"I know what you are thinking. How can I prove you wrong — now?"

There was no way for the Varn to prove him wrong, nor for him to prove the treachery behind the Varn proposal. The proof would come only with time, when the Terran-Varn cooperation had transformed Terrans into a slave race.

The Varn spoke again. *"You refuse to believe I am sincere?"*

"I would be a naïve fool to believe you."

"It will be too late to save Throon unless we act very quickly. I have told you why I am here. There is nothing more I can do to

convince you but be the first to show trust. When I switch on the lights it will be within your power to kill me."

*T*he Varn was gambling its life in a game in which he would be gambling the Plan and his race. It was a game he would end at the first sound of movement from the astrogator unit across the room. . . .

"*I have been here beside you all the time.*"

A furry paw brushed his face, claws flicked gently but grimly reminding along his throat.

He whirled and fired. He was too late — the Varn had already leaped silently away and the beam found only the bare floor. Then the lights came on, glaringly bright after the darkness, and he saw the Varn.

It was standing by the control board, its huge yellow eyes watching him. He brought the blaster into line with it, his finger on the firing stud. It waited, not moving or shrinking from what was coming. The translucent golden eyes looked at him and beyond him, as though they saw something not in the room. He wondered if it was in contact with its own kind on Johnny's World and was telling them it had made the gamble for high stakes, and had lost.

It was not afraid — not asking for mercy. . . .

The killing of it was suddenly an act without savor. It was something he would do in the immediate future but first he would let it live long enough to save Throon.

He motioned with the blaster and said, "Lead the way to the airlock."

"And afterward — you will kill me?"

"Lead the way," he repeated harshly.

It said no more but went obediently past him and trotted down the corridor like a great, black dog.

*H*e stood in the open airlock, the Varn against the farther wall where he had ordered it to stand. Throon was in the radiation chamber and he had held his first intelligible conversation with the natives that day.

The Varn was facing into the red-black gloom outside the lighted airlock, where the departing natives could be heard crossing the glade. *"Their thoughts no longer hold fear and suspicion,"* it said. *"The misunderstanding is ended."*

He raised the muzzle of the blaster in his hand. The black head lifted and the golden eyes looked up at him.

"I made you no promise," he said.

"I could demand none."

"I can't stop to take you back to your own world and I can't leave you alive on this one — with what you've learned from my mind you would have the natives build the Varn a disintegrator-equipped space fleet equal to our own ships."

"We want only to go with you."

He told it what he wanted it to know before he killed it, wondering why he should care:

"I would like to believe you are sincere — and you know why I don't dare to. Trusting a telepathic race would be too dangerous. The Varn would know everything we knew and only the Varn would be able to communicate with each new alien race. We would have to believe what the Varn told us — we would have to trust the Varn to see for us and speak for us and not deceive us as we went across the galaxy. And then, in the end, Terrans would no longer be needed except as a subject race. They would be enslaved.

"We would have laid the groundwork for an empire — the Varn Empire."

There was a silence, in which his words hung like something cold and invisible between them.

Then the Varn asked, very quietly:

"Why is the Plan failing?"

"You already know," he said. "Because of the barrier — the communication barrier that causes aliens to misunderstand the intentions of Exploration men and fear them."

"There is no communication barrier between you and I — yet you fear me and are going to kill me."

"I have to kill you. You represent a danger to my race."

"Isn't that the same reason why aliens kill Exploration men?"

He did not answer and its thought came, quickly, *"How does an Exploration man appear to the natives of alien worlds?"*

How did he appear?. . . He landed on their world in a ship that could smash it into oblivion; he stepped out of his ship carrying weapons that could level a city; he represented irresistible power for destruction and he trusted no one and nothing.

And in return he hoped to find welcome and friendship and cooperation. . . .

"There," the Varn said, *"is your true barrier — your own distrust and suspicion. You, yourselves, create it on each new world. Now you are going to erect it between my race and yours by*

killing me and advising the Exploration Board to quarantine my world and never let another ship land there."

Again there was a silence as he thought of what the Varn had said and of what it had said earlier: *"We are a very old race. . . ."* There was wisdom in the Varn's analysis of the cause of the Plan's failure and with the Varn to vanquish the communication stalemate, the new approach could be tried. They could go a long way together, men and Varn, a long, long way. . . .

Or they could create the Varn Empire . . . and how could he know which it would be?

How could anyone know — except the telepathic Varn?

The muzzle of the blaster had dropped and he brought it back up. He forced the dangerous indecision aside, knowing he would have to kill the Varn at once or he might weaken again, and said harshly to it:

"The risk is too great. I want to believe you — but all your talk of trust and good intentions is only talk and my race would be the only one that had to trust."

He touched the firing stud as the last thought of the Varn came:

"Let me speak once more."

He waited, the firing stud cold and metallic under his finger.

"You are wrong. We have already set the example of faith in you by asking to go with you. I told you we did not intend to hurt your brother and I told you we saw the stars only as the little wild animals saw them. The years in the dark caves — you do not understand —"

The eyes of the Varn looked into his and beyond him; beautiful, expressionless, like polished gold.

"The Varn are blind."

THE END

www.ingramcontent.com/pod-product-compliance
Lightning Source LLC
Chambersburg PA
CBHW031905170626
46807CB00004B/1911